GUNK
ALIENS
THE SEWERS CRISIS

Collect all the books in the *GUNK Aliens* series!

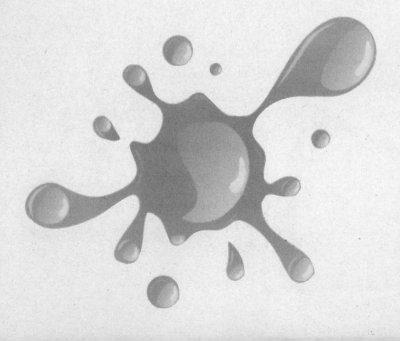

JONNY MOON

GUNK ALIENS
THE SEWERS CRISIS

HarperCollins *Children's Books*

First published in paperback in Great Britain by HarperCollins *Children's Books* 2009
HarperCollins Children's Books is a division of HarperCollinsPublishers Ltd
77-85 Fulham Palace Road, Hammersmith, London W6 8JB

The HarperCollins website address is:

www.harpercollins.co.uk

1

Copyright © HarperCollins 2009
Illustrations by Vincent Vigla
Illustrations © HarperCollins 2009

ISBN: 978-0-00-731097-5

Printed and bound in England by Clays Ltd, St Ives plc

Special thanks to Colin Brake,
GUNGE agent extraordinaire.

A long time ago, in a galaxy far, far away, a bunch of slimy aliens discovered the secret to clean, renewable energy...

... Snot!

(Well, OK, clean-*ish*.)

There was just one problem. The best snot came from only one kind of creature.

Humans.

And humans were very rare. Within a few years, the aliens had used up all the best snot in their solar system.

That was when the **Galactic Union of Nasty Killer Aliens (GUNK)** was born. Its mission: to find human life and drain its snot. Rockets were sent to the four corners of the universe, each carrying representatives from the major alien races. Three of those rockets were never heard from again. But one of them landed on a planet quite simply *full* of humans.

CHAPTER ONE

Jack Brady was worried.

By rights he should have been as happy as Larry – whoever Larry was. It was the first day of the summer holidays. No more school for six weeks! Jack should have been full of joy and excitement but instead he was anxious. He had unfinished business to deal with before he could enjoy the holiday.

For months now Jack had been engaged in a top-secret mission as an operative of GUNGE – a covert group of agents engaged in the fight to protect the planet from aliens. Along with his friends Oscar and Ruby, Jack and his robot dog Snivel (in reality a shape-changing alien-trap) had already captured three dangerous aliens but his GUNGE contact – a man known only as Bob – had told him that there were four aliens at large on Earth. Jack knew that it would soon be time to go after Number Four.

He just hoped he and his friends would be ready.

After three exciting alien-hunting adventures, Jack was still amazed at how lucky he had been to be chosen for this special work. After all, Jack was just an ordinary boy. Well, OK, he was a genius and an inventor as well but he was still pretty ordinary at heart. He went to school, had to clean his room when his mum told him to and loved hanging out with his friends – all pretty normal activities for a ten-year-old.

Jack's best mate Oscar lived in the house whose garden backed onto his own, and they shared the tree house at the bottom of both their gardens. Oscar was completely different to Jack. Where Jack was a thinker Oscar was definitely more of a do-er. If anything involved going very fast, or very high, or if it was in any way dangerous or risky then Oscar was always first in line.

When Jack had first been contacted by the mysterious Bob he had soon told Oscar all about the threat of the GUNK Aliens and why they wanted humankind's snot.

At first Oscar had laughed. Snot? But Jack had been entirely serious. Snot was like gold to the

GUNK Aliens. It was the most precious resource of all: the raw material from which they could create endless energy. All of the aliens' technology was powered by snot – but they had exhausted the natural supplies in their own galaxies, and now they needed a new source...

Four alien races, deeply suspicious of each other, had formed an alliance to search far and wide into the depths of space to find the energy source they all needed. The alliance was called the Galactic Union of Nasty Killer Aliens and their mission was simple: to boldly go to the four corners of the universe to seek out snot wherever it could be found.

The four alien races all really hated and distrusted each other so they made sure each scout ship had just one crew member from

each race. In addition each crew member had
a separate piece of the Blower – a pan-
dimensional signalling device that could
summon the mass invasion fleets of all four
species. Only with all four parts
of the Blower could such a
signal be sent. It was a kind of

insurance policy, forcing the four aliens to work together and ensuring that none of them tried to betray the alliance and keep any snot they found for their own kind alone.

Bob – and now Jack – worked for GUNGE (the General Under-Committee for the Neutralisation of Gruesome Extra-terrestrials). This was a human organisation with one mission: to prevent alien invasion of Earth. Bob had explained to Jack that one of the alien scout ships had discovered Earth and found it populated with *millions* of little snot-factories: the human race.

Luckily, before they could act on their discovery, the aliens had managed to crash their ship. The four aliens – and their respective parts of the Blower – had been scattered in all directions. Jack's job, as an agent of GUNGE, was to find the aliens, trap them using Snivel and secure the components of the Blower.

Jack and his
friends had
already
captured three
aliens: a
Squillibloat, a
Burrapong and a
Flartibug, but there
was one more to complete the set. Jack just
knew that this last one would be the grossest,
most disgusting of all. But why hadn't Bob
made contact yet? It had been weeks now
since Jack had last heard from the GUNGE
controller. Every day of the last agonising
week of the summer term – which seemed to
drag on for ever – Jack had walked home
from school hoping to hear Bob's voice from
each postbox, cash point and
rubbish bin he passed but it
never came. Even Snivel didn't

seem to know where Bob was.

In actual fact Bob was exactly where Jack might have expected him to be – in his top secret base. The problem was that the base was both mobile and transdimensional – which was why it had on previous occasions been located in a park bin, a postbox and a cash point. The energy needed to maintain such a blatant attack on the laws of physics was enormous, however, and so Bob's base spent most of the time at normal size, hidden within an anonymous grey warehouse in an industrial estate on the edge of town.

Although boring and featureless from the outside, the inside of the base was dark, mysterious and full of alien technology. It also contained a long dark corridor of glass-walled cells. In three of these cells, the captured aliens were being held in suspended animation. At the far end of the corridor was a glass shelved trophy cabinet with four display spaces. The Blower parts that the children had obtained from the Squillibloat, the Burrapong and the Flartibug were illuminated on three of the platforms. Just one platform remained dark and unoccupied.

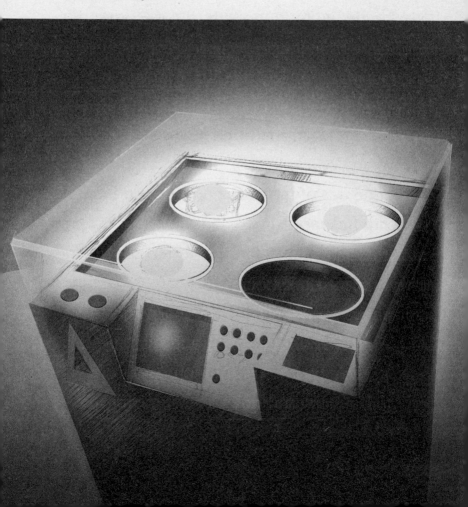

Bob walked down the corridor checking that the correct nutrients were being fed to the three aliens. He stopped and looked into the fourth, empty cell.

Room for one more, Bob thought to himself, *and then it's all over.*

He began to laugh, amused at some private joke. He laughed and laughed and laughed, until he was bent double and was wheezing from uncontrollable laughter. Abruptly he stopped and pulled himself together. Wiping a tear from his eye he headed out of the dark corridor and back to his control room. It was time for the final act of the drama to begin. He had to get the kids involved for one last mission.

In the control room he activated a screen and tuned into a local news broadcast. Zana Perkins smiled sweetly at the camera and concluded her report.

"Let's hope that Trixie the poodle finds her way home very soon. This is Zana Perkins  from Greenwick Parkway, back to you in the studio, Lorna," she trilled in her most excited voice.

The cameraman waved a hand to indicate that they were off-air. Instantly Zana's smile disappeared.

News items about missing dogs. That was what her life had come to. As if she cared that five dogs had vanished from the same estate in a single week. Big deal.

And having to hand back to Lorna in the studio left a sour taste in her mouth. That job – anchoring the news in the studio – should have been hers, instead she was back on the road, doing silly local news stories of minor importance. Zana's career was going into a nose dive and she had to do something to stop it. A few months ago she had been the host of a popular zoo-based programme *Animal Ark* and when she got the chance to move to news she had jumped at the opportunity.

Unfortunately things had not worked out. Twice she had encountered Jack and his friends and, in doing so, she had stumbled on an amazing story of alien invaders but, despite her best efforts, she kept failing to get any *proof* on camera. Zana knew better than anyone else that if it wasn't on telly, no one would pay any attention.

Zana handed the microphone back to the cameraman. "I'm off then," she told him, "give me a call if any more dogs go missing."

Zana stalked off, walking past a newspaper

stand on which was displayed the heading, 'FIFTH PET DISAPPEARS!'

The cameraman watched her go and shook his head. He couldn't work out Zana at all. He was used to the peculiar behaviour of on-screen talent but this was something else. Every spare moment, whenever she wasn't actually on camera, Zana was off working on some secret project of her own. Whatever it was, she didn't want to talk about it. He had asked her about it once but she'd just changed the subject.

He watched as Zana walked off into the distance, wondering where she was going.

Jack put down the remote-controlled car he had been taking apart (with the intention of using its frame for the base of a new automated shopping trolley he had designed) and looked over at Snivel, who was sitting on the carpet in his room. A mistake in the manufacturing of Snivel had left him with three eyes, which got

him a lot of strange looks when they were out. Snivel was always trying to find ways to keep the third eye closed so that people wouldn't notice it. Unfortunately the effort to do this caused other malfunctions.

PARP!

"Snivel!"

"Sorry," said Snivel, waving a paw in a

desperate effort to make the smell he had just produced disappear again. "Just trying to close this eye." He closed his third eye, then fell over.

PARP! He farted again.

"Come on," sighed Jack, getting to his feet, "let's get some air, and while we're at it we can try and find Bob."

"The park?" said Snivel.

Jack nodded. The park. The place he had first encountered Bob. Where better to start the search?

Zana had one thought in her head. Whatever was going on with the alien monsters it was all connected to the three kids that she'd met previously – Jack, Oscar and Ruby. With the school holidays underway there was just one obvious place that they might be found – the park.

The park was a big open space in the middle of the town. It had a boating pond, tennis courts, a maze and even a little café. It was to this last feature that Zana headed. She took a seat on the terrace, ordered a large coffee and settled down to wait.

Nearby, unseen by Zana, a squirrel climbed down a tree trunk and sat on its haunches on the ground. With unnatural smoothness it then turned its head – all the way round! It looked uncannily like a security camera sweeping the area. Which wasn't surprising, because that was basically what it was. The squirrel was really a robot – one of Bob's many agents in the field. With a

low whirring sound, its mechanical eyes
zoomed in on Zana.

Back in his base, Bob frowned as the feed
from Squirrel-Cam showed him the young TV
reporter sipping her coffee. This was a
complication. He recognised the young
woman from previous missions. Whether by
luck or by judgement she was always in the
wrong place at the wrong time. It was clear
that she was beginning to put two and two
together and getting perilously close to four.
Bob issued orders to the squirrel to keep a
close robotic eye on Zana. If it looked as if
she was going to be a problem, then they
would have to deal with her. The plan was
about to come to fruition and nothing could
be allowed to get in the way.

No matter what the cost.

CHAPTER TWO

Jack was beginning to wonder if coming to the park had been a mistake. He and Snivel had been walking around for what seemed like hours but there was no sign of anything that might contain Bob.

Jack didn't fully understand how Bob got himself into such tiny places – he assumed that GUNGE had got hold of some alien technology somewhere along the way – but every time Bob had shown himself to Jack, he had been inside something small, and whatever else Bob was, he did seem to be a creature of habit. So it seemed likely that Jack would find him in a similar place this time. Maybe he'd be in a fire extinguisher? Or a vending machine?

In fact, now Jack thought about it, that was just about all they did know about Bob. They'd never even seen him face to face. For all they knew he could have been around all the time. Perhaps the park keeper was really Bob?! Jack shook his head. He was letting his imagination run away with him. Things were complicated enough without him imagining hidden people in disguise spying on him all the time.

Suddenly Snivel stood bolt upright and his third eye – which he tried very hard to

keep shut when out and about – snapped
open and glowed a strange red colour.

"What is it? What have you seen?" asked
Jack.

Snivel didn't answer but just started running
across the grass, trailing his lead behind him.
Nearby, the park keeper was sweeping up
some rubbish on the path and when he saw
Snivel speeding across the grass he threw
down his brush and shouted.

"Oi! Dogs must be kept on a lead!"

"Sorry," said Jack, chasing after his dog. "He is on a lead, I'm just not holding the other end, that's all."

"Keep off the grass!" screamed the park keeper and started to follow him but then stopped when he realised he was about to step onto the grass himself. For a long moment he stood there like an inelegant ballet dancer – one foot planted on the path, one hovering over the grass which, by his own park law, was not to be trodden on. Meanwhile, the reason for Snivel's action had become clear to Jack. His dog had seen a squirrel.

But not just any squirrel – it was the robot squirrel that had led them to Bob on a previous occasion. The squirrel, seeing Snivel bearing down on him, had immediately jumped up and started running.

On the café terrace Zana looked over the top of the newspaper she was hiding behind and watched with amazement as one of her targets ran straight past her, chasing a dog, which was chasing a squirrel. The trio disappeared around the side of the café and then – a few moments later – emerged on the other side. Zana got to her feet and slipped some dark glasses on. Completing her effort at disguise with a large floppy-brimmed sun hat, she set off to follow the chase.

The squirrel was heading back across the grass towards the spot where the park keeper was still performing his one-man ballet. It glanced back and saw that Snivel was just behind. Not looking where it was going, the squirrel barrelled directly into the park keeper, sending him toppling to the ground. Without missing a beat, the squirrel jumped up and

ran on. Snivel launched into the air like a horse jumping a fence at the Grand National and cleared the park keeper who was sprawled face first in the grass. Jack tried to do the same but mistimed his jump and

ended up executing more of a hop, skip and a jump using the park keeper's bum as a springboard along the way. Spitting out a mouthful of grass the park keeper got to his feet just as Zana reached him.

"Hold it right there," he ordered and Zana pulled up. The park keeper looked behind Zana. It was very obvious where she had been. Her high-heeled shoes had left a series of holes across the perfect lawn. "That's why it says keep off the grass," said the park keeper, fuming.

"Oops," said Zana, not really looking at the angry man in uniform. Zana's focus was in the distance where she could see Jack disappearing into the entrance to the hedge maze.

Jack had solved the maze years ago, with the help of a remote-control aeroplane and a video camera, so he had no problems moving directly through the winding pathways to get to the middle, where a couple of park benches and a little flower display were all the reward you got for making it successfully

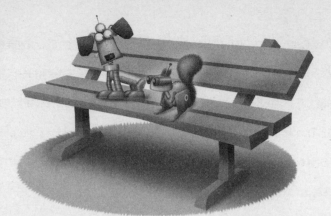

through the maze. When he got there he found Snivel and the squirrel sitting beside each other on one of the benches.

"Ah, there you are," said Bob's voice, coming from the squirrel.

"Bob? Are you in the squirrel now?" he asked.

"Of course not," said Bob, sounding a little impatient. "I'm just using the squirrel to communicate. There are eyes and ears everywhere. We need to be vigilant. It's possible the GUNK Aliens have recruited agents in the local media..."

Jack cast a quick glance around him. There didn't seem to be any cameras around here.

"I think we're OK at the centre of the maze," said Jack.

"Exactly. That's why I led you in here, of course. Now listen carefully..."

"Alien number four?" Jack asked, anticipating what Bob was about to say.

"This will go much better if you keep your mouth shut and listen," insisted Bob in a tetchy tone. Jack glanced at Snivel and raised his eyebrows. Bob was certainly in an odd mood today. Snivel just shrugged (a manoeuvre he was still working on) and fell over.

"What's wrong with Snivel?" asked Bob, through the squirrel. "Is he running low on snot?"

Even though Snivel worked for GUNGE, he had been made using captured alien

technology, so he ran on the same thing GUNK used to power all their devices.

Snot!

"No," said Jack. "He's just trying to shrug. He's not very good at it."

"Actually," said Snivel, "I could do with some snot. People don't have as many colds in the summer. I'm starving!"

Jack sighed. "I blew my nose for you this morning!"

"Hmm," said Snivel, grudgingly. "Not much more than a mouthful, though."

"Yes, well," said Bob, interrupting. "As long as you're not about to break down on us, I'm sure you'll be all right. Shall we get on with the briefing?"

"Yes, sir," said Snivel, sarcastically.

"Oh, good," said Bob, just as sarcastically. Then he took a breath, before continuing in a much more serious tone. "The final alien is the most dangerous of the lot. Snivel will be data-uploaded with all the information you need. But you must be careful. This creature is smart. If it realises that we have the other parts of the Blower, then it has the intelligence to use Earth radio-telescope technology to get a message home without it. But his part of the Blower is the key signal generator: if we get that safely away from him, it won't matter what technology he begs, steals or borrows, he still won't be able to send the right encoded signal."

Suddenly there was a crashing noise nearby and Zana, still wearing her dark glasses and big hat, stumbled into the clearing at the centre of the maze.

"Were you talking to that squirrel?" she demanded, pointing at the squirrel-bot, which immediately disappeared through a hole in the nearest hedge.

"What squirrel?" said Jack innocently.

"The squirrel that was just there! I heard you talking to it!"

"How could I be talking to a squirrel I didn't know was there?"

Zana stamped her foot. "I heard voices. A man's voice."

Jack smiled, as if slowly realising something. "Oh, I was listening to the radio," he explained.

"What radio?"

Jack rummaged in his pocket. As usual bits and pieces of various projects were in there. He pulled out a small plastic box.

"This radio," he said. "Amazing how small they are these days, isn't it?"

Quickly slipping the box (which in reality

held a memory card for his camera) back into his pocket, Jack stepped past Zana and led Snivel back through the maze.

Zana sat down on one of the benches and fumed. She knew she'd heard voices, and more than that, she knew what the voices had said. Aliens. She was on the right track. And that boy – Jack – was the key. She got to her feet, determined not to let the trail run cold.

She moved out of the central clearing and faced a choice – left or right. Which way had she come in? "Help!" she cried "I think I'm lost." There was no reply. She called louder. "Help me!"

Outside the maze the park keeper raised his head at the scream for help. He then went back to his work, patiently filling in the hundreds of holes the woman had made in his lawn with fresh soil and grass seed. Maybe when he'd finished repairing the damage she caused he might go and rescue her from the maze.

Then again, maybe he wouldn't.

CHAPTER THREE

In the branches of the tree that grew at the foot of Oscar's garden, and which overhung both his and Jack's garden, there was a tree house. In fact it was more than just a tree house. It was Jack's workshop, Oscar's bolt hole and, unofficially, the headquarters of Jack's branch of GUNGE. It was actually a proper garden shed which Oscar's dad had won in a competition. It had needed a crane to install it in the tree and it was, by anyone's standards, a spectacular tree house.

Right now it was hosting a meeting of GUNGE agents – Jack had summoned Oscar and Ruby to an urgent briefing. Unfortunately Oscar and Ruby had a very different understanding of *urgent* to Jack and it was nearly lunchtime when the pair finally arrived.

"Where have you been?" asked Jack from his workbench where he had been fiddling with his latest invention while waiting.

"Relax, it's the summer hols, there's no rush," replied Oscar.

"Have you seen the sun out there? It's a gorgeous day! We should be out there having fun not stuck in here," added Ruby.

Jack just glared at them. "I've heard from Bob. Snivel's been uploaded with the latest mission data for us."

Ruby and Oscar exchanged a look and sighed. "OK then, let's get it over with," said Oscar.

Snivel activated his hidden hologram projector and a green-tinged beam of light emerged from his third eye and formed a three-dimensional screen. On the screen a giant alien cow-like creature was displayed.

"That doesn't look too dangerous," commented Ruby.

"That's a Mooville, a giant cow-like creature from the Planet Goldtop. They are so large they blot out the sun, which means that it's permanently dark on the surface of the planet."

"And that's the fourth GUNK Alien? A giant cow? That's not going to be hard to find," said Oscar.

Snivel shook his head, making the hologram wobble.

"The fourth GUNK Alien is the Slurrisnoat. They also live on Goldtop. But they like it dark and smelly… They live in… well, burrows."

There was something Jack didn't like about the way Snivel had hesitated. "What do you mean *burrows?*" he asked. "This is going to be bad, isn't it?"

"These burrows – are they under the surface of the planet?" asked Ruby hopefully.

"Er… not exactly. Actually, they're in the Mooville's giant cow-pats," explained Snivel. "They dig deep into the poo and that's where they make their homes," he added.

"Oh, gross," muttered Ruby.

"At least this one won't be hard to find," said Jack with a grim smile.

Oscar and Ruby both looked at him.

"Think about it. The Slurrisnoat likes it warm, dark and full of poo. So where's it going to hang out?"

"In a toilet?" wondered Oscar.

"In the sewers, of course." Jack told him. "Where do you think it all goes when you flush a toilet? Down the drains and into the sewers."

There was a long silence while each of them allowed this to sink in.

"So we need to go down the sewers to look for this Slurrisnoat?" said Ruby after a bit.

Jack nodded.

"And just poke around in all that... stuff... until we find it?" said Oscar.

Jack nodded again.

There was another silence.

"It really is a very lovely day out there," said Ruby eventually.

"Be a shame to waste a day like that underground," added Oscar.

"You know what the summer hols can be like. Week after week of rain. We really should enjoy the sun while we can," Ruby continued.

Jack knew what they meant. It was the start of the holidays and the sun was shining and...

"It's not like we haven't already got the other three aliens, is it? This one on his own can't be that dangerous." Jack realised with a pang of guilt that it was *his* voice joining the others in finding excuses not to go after the Slurrisnoat straightaway. He tried to ignore his memory of Bob's final warning. What harm could a short delay do, anyway?

"Did I tell you I've got a new BMX?" said Oscar suddenly.

"Cool," said Ruby speedily. "If only we had a half-pipe to ride in."

"I think we could rig something up," said Jack, joining in with their enthusiasm, "and perhaps we could give the bike a little extra poke, add a motor or something..."

"Brilliant," said Oscar.

"Awesome," said Ruby.

"So it's agreed – the search for the Slurrisnoat can wait," said Jack.

"Just till tomorrow," added Ruby.

"Or the day after," suggested Oscar.

Snivel cleared his throat. "Can I just say–" he began, but Jack cut him off.

"Sorry," he said, "no votes for dogs."

Elsewhere, Bob was pacing about his control centre, fuming silently. Why had nothing happened yet? Did those children not understand the urgency of the situation? If the Slurrisnoat wasn't stopped soon, everything that Bob had been working towards would be for nothing.

The Squirrel-Cam had been watching the children all day. Far from planning their next move they seemed to be more interested in playing in the sun.

Bob growled to himself. If only he didn't need the kids...

The Squirrel-Cam was not the only observer watching Jack, Oscar and Ruby playing in Oscar's garden – Zana was also on the case. Wearing her usual disguise of dark glasses

and floppy hat Zana had spent the day walking up and down the road where Oscar lived, casting glances over the fence to check on what the children were doing. Mostly they seemed to be getting wet.

Jack and his fellow GUNGE agents were having a really fun afternoon. Hour after hour went by without them noticing as they hung out in Oscar's garden. Oscar and Ruby played with the new BMX bike and with some

of Jack's remote-control devices, while Jack
sketched ambitious plans for a half-pipe and
other stunt bike equipment to be assembled
and built over the rest of the summer. Snivel,
unable to get a word in edgeways, went to
sleep under the tree.

At lunchtime, Oscar's mum provided them
with some sandwiches and crisps and then
later she disappeared into the garage and
emerged with a massive
inflatable swimming pool. While
Oscar and Jack filled the pool

Ruby nipped off home to collect her swimming costume and soon the three of them were splashing about like any normal kid on a hot summer's afternoon, all thoughts of aliens and GUNGE completely forgotten.

They played all afternoon. Jack kept popping up to the tree house to fetch various inventions for them to use, including his snorkel mask with integrated radios, his clockwork surfboard and his turbo-charged super soakers. These were the biggest hit of all – literally. With Jack's use of compressed air to add extra welly these were the best and most powerful super soakers ever seen on the planet. Jack and Oscar managed to knock Ruby completely off her feet.

"Oi!" she shouted in mock annoyance.

Zana was getting frustrated. What on earth

were the kids up
to? Was all this
shouting and
water-play
really a cover-
up for something
more important.
Every time she passed
the garden, she had noticed
that Jack was busy sketching things in a big
sketchbook. If only she could get a closer look
at whatever it was he was designing. Grabbing
her binoculars she crept closer to the garden
fence. An alley ran along the side of Oscar's
house, and there was a low wall on one side
which Zana realised she could climb to get a
better look. Wobbling a little she managed to
get herself on to the top of the
wall. Carefully she put the
binoculars to her face and

looked over the fence into the back garden.

In front of her, with their backs towards her, were the two boys. Beyond them was the girl holding something that looked like a green plastic stick in her hand. Zana could see that it was attached to a long thin plastic tube that ran back towards the house. Before she could react to this sight, Ruby activated the release on the hose and a flume of freezing cold water shot towards the boys, who ducked, leaving

the aqua-attack to hit Zana full in the face.

Zana fell off the wall into the alley and landed in some rubbish. The hose had been even more powerful than the super soakers and she was drenched to the skin. Dripping like a drowned rat she limped back to her car, utterly miserable.

Ruby never even saw that she had soaked the poor journalist – she was too busy laughing and redirecting the hose to shower both Oscar and Jack. This was what summer was for. Getting wet and having fun.

The three of them laughed and screamed and had the best, wildest afternoon they'd had all year. And not one of them mentioned aliens, not even once.

Little did they know, but it was going to be their last chance to play in the sunshine for quite a long time…

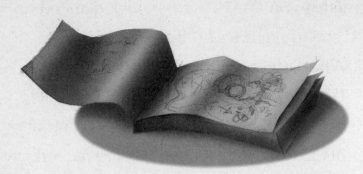

cHAPTER FOUR

With it being the school holidays, Jack was allowed to stay up later than usual and found himself still downstairs with his mum when the local news came on. He was busy with his sketch book, working on ever more ambitious plans to transform Oscar's garden into a combination of a water theme park and a BMX stunt bike arena.

"Oh, that's terrible," said Jack's mum, at

something on the TV screen. Jack glanced up and saw a picture of a dog on the screen.

"What's wrong with the dog?" he asked.

"It's gone missing," explained his mum. She told him that according to the news a number of cats and dogs had gone missing recently in mysterious circumstances, all in the same part of town. Jack asked which part of town.

"Up past the industrial park, where the river bends," said Jack's mum.

Jack swallowed hard, as a horrible thought came into his head.

"Sort of near the sewage works?" he suggested.

His mum thought a moment and then nodded. "Yes, I suppose it is."

Jack put down his sketch book and jumped up. "I think I'll go to bed now," he announced and rushed out of the room.

Upstairs in his room Jack found Snivel with his nose jammed into one of the USB ports on his computer. All three eyes were blinking rapidly and glowing red.

"Snivel, I need you!"

Snivel closed his eyes, shivered and pulled back from the computer. His nose, which had transformed itself into a USB-shaped connector, snapped back to its more usual shape.

"Sorry," said Snivel. "I was downloading

everything I could find about the Slurrisnoat."

Jack was confused. "You Googled it?"

Snivel shook his head. "Of course not. I just used the internet connection to access the GUNGE databanks."

"Is it likely that this Slurrisnoat eats cats and dogs?" asked Jack, a serious expression on his face.

If Snivel was surprised at this question, he didn't show it.

"Yes, of course, very likely. The Slurrisnoat just *lives* in poo – it doesn't eat it. It eats mammals."

"Mammals like cats and dogs?"

"As snacks, yes. But it really prefers something a little larger."

Jack's eyes widened as the significance of what Snivel was saying sank in. He sat down in front of the computer and began typing.

"I'm e-mailing the others," he told Snivel. "I don't think we can delay looking for this Slurrisnoat a day longer."

The next morning Ruby and Oscar both arrived on time for once. They climbed into the tree house and found a very serious-looking Jack waiting for them. He quickly explained about the missing cats and dogs.

Oscar was immediately concerned. "You mean Princess might be in danger?" he asked. Princess was Oscar's cat.

"You don't even *like* Princess," said Jack. "None of us do. She's a vicious bundle of fur and claws."

"Yeah, but Mum would be really upset if anything happened to her," replied Oscar.

"I think we've got bigger problems than missing cats and dogs to worry about," suggested Ruby. "Am I right?"

Jack nodded. "Snivel says the Slurrisnoat eats mammals, the bigger the better. Cats and dogs won't satisfy it for long, it'll seek bigger prey." He paused. "*Human* prey."

Ruby and Oscar exchanged horrified looks.

"You mean it'll start to eat people?" stammered Oscar.

"Definitely," said Snivel. "After cows, you're the biggest mammals around. And the Slurrisnoat doesn't eat cows. They think of the giant Moovilles from their home planet as gods. So cows are sacred to them."

"Well, that's just great," said Oscar.

"How are we going to stop an alien monster that eats people?" demanded Ruby. "If we go down the sewers looking for it, we'll just end up staying for dinner. And *we'll* be on the menu!"

"The Slurrisnoat does have a

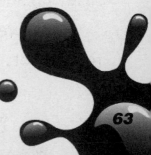

weakness," said Snivel, "it loves poo so it hates anything clean. It really, really hates soap."

"Must be a boy then," muttered Ruby.

"There's no need to be like that," said Oscar and Jack together.

"So all we have to do is get inside the sewers, stumble around up to our knees in filthy sewage, find a man-eating monster and get close enough to it to give it a good scrubbing with soap?" asked Ruby sarcastically.

Snivel nodded.

"That's about the size of it," said Jack.

Ruby got up from the floor cushion she was sitting on. "Well, I've got a lesson to get to," she announced. "When you've come up with a plan, let me know. But it had better not involve me splashing through poo-filled water!"

As she got up her jacket flapped open and the boys saw that she was wearing a leotard.

"Has your mum finally got you doing ballet then?" asked Oscar, laughing.

Ruby pulled the jacket around her. "Yeah right!"

Ruby loved to try new and exciting sports but her mother was less keen. For her mum's sake Ruby usually told her that she was doing ballet lessons or something equally safe rather than the truth.

"So what are you really doing? Rock climbing? Potholing? Skydiving?"

"I'm learning to jet-ski!" she explained.

"Cool!" said Oscar, who shared Ruby's adrenaline-addiction. "But not your cup of tea at all, Jack, eh?" Oscar nudged Jack with his elbow. Jack was a great ideas guy but not exactly a man of action.

In fact, Jack was thinking about an idea right now. Oscar and Ruby recognised the look on their friend's face.

"Actually the jet-ski thing sounds rather interesting. Can we come and watch?"

Ruby looked surprised, but she shrugged. "Why not?"

The three of them walked in virtual silence to the local lake. No one wanted to mention the threat of the Slurrisnoat, but with Snivel's warning about the creature's inevitable move to eating people ringing in their ears it was hard to put the matter out of their minds.

As they walked, each deep in their own thoughts, none of them noticed that they were being followed by a small yellow car being driven by a woman wearing a large floppy sun hat and dark glasses.

Zana drove slowly, pulling in now and again to let other traffic go at a more normal speed. Despite the washout of yesterday she was determined to keep a close eye on the three children, feeling certain that they would lead her to the aliens and the story that would make her the most famous journalist on the planet.

Finally, the children reached the lake which appeared to be their destination and Zana parked in a quiet spot nearby. She had binoculars so she wouldn't need to get too close. She found a spot near the water to settle down and watch. Sprawling out, face down, she put the binoculars to her eyes and focused on the girl who, it appeared, was about to have a jet-ski lesson.

Oscar and Jack enjoyed watching Ruby whizzing around the lake, but for different reasons. Oscar just loved the action of it, and wished he could have a go. Jack, however, was just watching the way the jet-ski moved smoothly over the water. As he watched, an idea began to form in his head. Ruby's lesson concluded with some spectacular jumps. The jet-ski hit some ramps and came down with a massive splash each time. There was a circuit of ramps, each higher than the last. On the final jump the splash was enormous, sending a huge wave of water crashing onto the nearby land.

Ruby pulled up at the jetty where Oscar and Jack were waiting for her.

"What did you think?" she asked.

"Awesome," they said in unison.

Zana couldn't believe it. One moment she had been watching the girl zoom around the lake and the next moment she'd disappeared from view. Then, before she had a chance to find her again in her binocular view, a massive wave of water had come crashing down, landing precisely where Zana was lying.

Zana was soaked through. Again!

She got to her feet, shivering and dripping,

her floppy sun hat a shapeless blob on her head. She squelched back to her car with a furious expression on her face. *If I get wet one more time*, she thought to herself, *I'm going to give this whole thing up.*

cHAPTER FIVE

Back at the tree-house, Jack outlined his plan to the others.

"We need to get around the sewers without paddling through the sewage," he pointed out to them, "so we'll borrow a jet-ski from Ruby's club and I'll make a carrying platform for it to pull. We can use that to drive around the sewers."

He looked at Ruby and

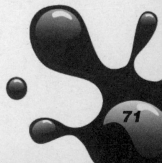

Oscar to see if they were with him so far. They both nodded.

"Then it's business as usual. Find the alien, grab the Blower bit, get Snivel into position then..."

"Shout out 'Activate Snivel Trap' and wham bam, it's all over," concluded Ruby.

"So how do we get into the sewers?" asked Oscar.

Jack grinned. "Remember we went to the water treatment plant when we were looking for the Burrapong?"

Oscar sighed. "We had to have that long tour of the place," he recalled.

"That's right, and during the tour I spotted a big intake pipe. We can get into the sewer system from there."

"And what about the Slurrisnoat – how do we defend ourselves?" asked Ruby.

"Using out super soakers," said Jack, "filled

with concentrated washing-up liquid."

Oscar and Ruby exchanged looks and nodded. "Let's do it!"

Zana had changed her clothes and returned to her surveillance of the children. She was relieved to see that they had all gathered in the tree house – which she could watch, with her binoculars, from the safety of the road.

Something was definitely happening. The children seemed to be making preparations for something. Zana was certain they were about to go on one of their alien hunts. She made sure she had everything she was going to need – stills camera, video camera, mobile phone with camera as a back-up. She also changed into some waterproof overalls – just in case. Finally she was ready. Just then the three children emerged onto the street. Each kid had a massive super soaker strapped to

their back. The boys were carrying what appeared to be a pair of wooden children's scooters, fixed together with struts and with the wheels removed. It looked like a series of inflatable arm bands had been stuck to the bottom of each scooter.

Zana turned on the engine of her car and began to follow them again. They appeared to be taking the same route as they had earlier in the day. They were going back to the lake.

The trio of children approached the jet-ski club. Lessons had finished for the day and everything was locked up. There was a large shed at the water's edge where the jet-skis were kept.

Ruby looked a little worried. "Isn't this ever so slightly

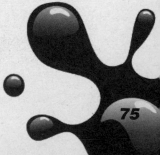

stealing?" she asked as Jack used a little gadget to crack the entrance code on the electronic door lock.

"Borrowing," said Jack, "and it is in the interests of saving the world. I'm sure Bob will be able to sort it out."

"And it *is* only for a few hours; we'll bring it back," added Oscar.

A moment later Jack had the door open
and they soon had a fully-fuelled jet-ski out
on the lake. Ruby watched carefully as the
boys fixed their improvised carrying platform
to the back of the vehicle and they had a
quick practice run. It worked like a dream.
The floats, once inflated, gave the scooters
just enough buoyancy and the scooter handle
bars helped Jack and Oscar keep their
balance while Ruby (and the jet-ski) dragged
them along.

Just in case, they had stolen lifejackets to wear as well. (Which is to say, they had *borrowed* lifejackets. Honest.)

"Now what – how do we get this to the intake pipe?" asked Ruby.

Jack got out a map. "The lake's fed by the river… *here*," he said, pointing to a spot on the map. "And if you follow the river for a mile or so we reach *here*… the intake pipe. So all we have to do is go upriver."

Ruby got back on her jet-ski. "Come on then, let's get going." The boys took up their positions.

Back in the jet-ski club's shed an automatic system noted that the lock had been open for fifteen minutes without the code being reset and a silent alarm was sounded. Five miles away in the local police station a red light began to flash on a massive map of the area. The police officer on duty looked up and reached for the radio...

In her little yellow car Zana was beginning to wonder where the kids had got to. She'd watched them heading towards the jet-ski club and assumed that they had forgotten something earlier but that had been twenty minutes ago and they hadn't come back yet.

Zana checked her local map. There was no other way out, apart from the path the children had taken. They had to come back the same way. Unless they'd gone across the lake. Surely they hadn't done that, had they?

With a sudden cold fear that her targets might have escaped, Zana jumped out of her car and headed down the path towards the clubhouse. She approached carefully, not

sure if the children were still in there. She could hear no voices. She crept closer still. She saw that the door to the clubhouse was open. It was dark inside, with no windows.

"Hello?" she called.

There was no answer. Using the light from her mobile phone as a torch Zana went inside. She tripped over something on the floor and stumbled onto her knees.

Suddenly a very bright torch light caught her in its beam. Shielding her eyes with her hand Zana turned around to face the torch-holder.

A second torch joined the first. With the additional light she could make out that the torch-holders were a man and a woman both of whom were wearing a familiar uniform.

"The police!" she cried out.

"Yes, we are, ma'am," said the policeman, "and you, my love, are under arrest!"

CHAPTER SIX

Ruby was proving to be a skilful jet-ski driver. She'd piloted them across the lake and into the river without any problems. Jack and Oscar had managed not to fall off the carrying platform once. Oscar was loving the thrill of the ride but Jack was finding the experience much harder. Snivel was sitting at his feet, waiting to capture another alien.

"Don't worry, Jack, it'll be all right," he

assured his master.

Jack's mobile bleeped and he reached into his pocket to pull it out.

"Text message," he told the others, "from Bob. He wants me to text him when we get the Slurrisnoat."

"He's getting a bit impatient, isn't he?" muttered Oscar.

"He says time is of the essence," said Jack, finishing reading the text.

"Well, we're going as fast as we can!" replied Ruby.

After a while they reached the intake pipe. It was protected by a giant grille but there was a mechanism to raise it to allow access and it was computerised. It took Snivel no time at all to access the system and unlock the mechanism, allowing Ruby to pilot their craft into the intake pipe. They each put on

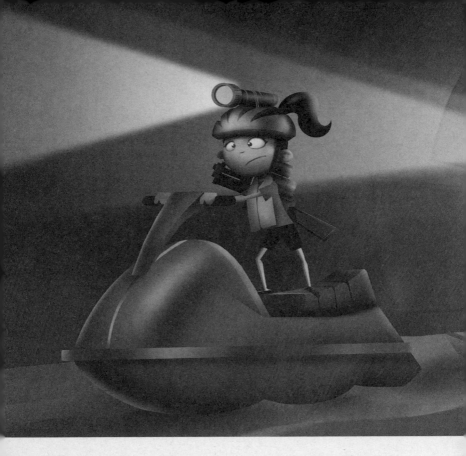

their safety helmets. These were simple bike helmets to which Jack had attached powerful torches, which they now switched on.

Oscar looked around at the inside of the huge pipe with fascination.

"Imagine what this place would be like drained," he suggested. "It would make an

awesome BMX site."

Ruby slowly drove the jet-ski deeper into the pipe. They reached junctions and had to make decisions about which way to go.

"Remember our route," Ruby told the boys, "we may need to come back this way in a hurry."

As they went further into the sewer system the water became gradually darker. And there were things floating in it. Things Jack *really* didn't want to look at too closely.

"Um... do you smell anything?" asked Jack eventually.

Oscar sniffed and gagged. "I think I smell everything!" he replied.

"Oh, God," said Ruby. "I think I'm going to hurl."

"Time for the nose clips," said Jack. He had provided each of them with a pair of nose clips and a filter, together he hoped these would protect them from the worst of the foul smells.

"What was that?" said Ruby suddenly. She switched off the jet-ski engine and listened. There was a scratching noise nearby. Something was moving in the shadows. Then something else moved. Without any further

warning the whole wall started to undulate.
Lots and lots of things were moving along the
lower part of the wall.

"Oh, rats!" shouted Ruby.

"What is it?" asked Oscar. "Forgotten
something?"

"No – I mean *rats*. Real rats. Loads of them,
coming this way."

The boys turned their torches and saw
exactly what Ruby meant. An
army of rats was streaming
down the walls of the pipe they

were in. Some were in the dirty water, swimming for their lives.

Ruby tried to switch on the jet-ski engine again. It refused to start. The boys watched in

horror as the wave of rats came closer. If they didn't start moving soon the rats would run right over them. Ruby tried again and this

time the engine fired into life. She shot forward towards the rats, which dived out of her way. In moments the rats had all passed them, as the kids roared forward in the opposite direction. When they were clear of the rats Ruby slowed again and turned back to the boys.

"What do you think they were running away from?"

Oscar and Jack looked at each other. "The Slurrisnoat!" they chorused.

Zana was not a happy woman, but at least she wasn't wet. What she was, however, was under arrest and locked in a police cell.

She heard the noise of a bolt being pulled back and the metal door of the cell squeaked open.

"About time," she said, "I'd like

a word with someone in charge."

"That's a coincidence, miss," said the policeman at the door, "someone in charge wants a word with you."

As a journalist Zana was used to conducting interviews, although she rarely had a room called an interview room in which to do it. And she was definitely more used to asking the questions than to answering them.

"Just tell us the truth," said the police officer sitting opposite her, "and I'm sure we can sort this business out."

Zana considered her position. How much of the truth should she really tell? She wasn't certain but she had a suspicion that if the told the police that she was following three children, it wouldn't go down very well. If she told them that she'd been following the children for days, it would probably be even worse. And if she told them why she was following the children – in an effort to discover the truth about aliens on Earth – then she'd probably get herself locked up in a padded cell!

No, despite the policeman's advice, this was no time for the truth, Zana decided.

She invented a much simpler story for the policeman, using her credentials as a journalist.

She'd heard a whisper that the missing cats and dogs might be connected to the lake and had been investigating when she'd heard some kind of break-in at the jet-ski club. When she had gone to check it out she'd found the door open. And that was just before the police arrived. The police were suspicious, but Zana had one strong piece of evidence on her side: she didn't have the missing jet-ski. Even the police had to admit that she'd have trouble hiding something so big if she really had stolen it.

After a few formalities and some paperwork Zana was reluctantly released from the police station and taken back to her car. She waved goodbye to the policemen who had given her a lift and went straight to her map. She knew now that the children must have gone across the lake – but where were they going to? She looked at the map carefully, traced the path of the river which fed the lake and then she saw it. The sewage works. She remembered the two aliens that she'd seen already – one at the zoo, one in the school kitchen. Both aliens seemed to like disgusting things. And what was more disgusting than sewage?

All she needed now was transport. Zana saw that there were lights on at the jet-ski club. The members must have been alerted by the police to the break-in. Zana set off to have a chat.

The tunnels were getting bigger and darker as Ruby and the boys went further and further into the sewers. They were also getting harder to navigate as more and more lumps of... matter filled the filthy water. Ruby had to slow the jet-

ski to a crawl in order to prevent quite so
much of the nasty stuff being thrown up as
they passed through.

Up ahead they could hear something
splashing.

Ruby took the engine right down and they moved on at an even slower speed. The pipe they were in was opening up into a much bigger space. They emerged into a sort of sewage crossroads. Half a dozen pipes met

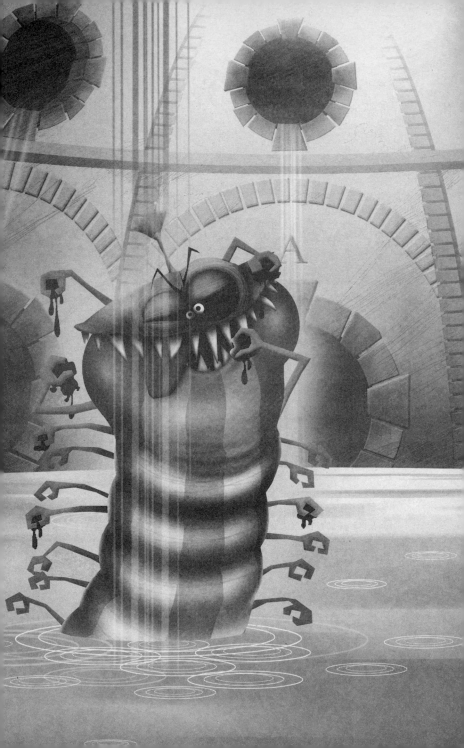

here in a gigantic hall and three or four other pipes came in higher up, making waterfalls of revolting brown sludge. Beneath one of these 'waterfalls', bathing in the fresh poo as it poured down, was the foulest creature any of the children had ever seen. It was a big fat maggoty alien, with hundreds of tiny three-fingered hands over its entire body. The hands were all busy rubbing the foul poo-filled water into its skin like the world's most disgusting moisturiser.

"Look!" said Ruby pointing. Hanging around its neck was a glowing ring – the Blower part.

The three of them reached for their super soakers.

"Who you gonna call?" muttered Jack, bringing the weapon up into a firing position.

"Alien Busters!" shouted Oscar and Ruby with glee.

cHAPTER SEVEN

The jet-ski club members had been very friendly, especially when Zana had explained that she might have a lead on whoever had stolen the jet-ski from them but, nevertheless, they had been reluctant to lend her one to continue her pursuit. Instead they had offered her an inflatable power boat, which was better than nothing.

After a quick lesson in how to steer the

vessel Zana set off and, after a little while, reached the intake pipe for the sewer system. She noted that the grille gate was in the open position proving that the children had already come this way. Bracing herself for the stench, she set off into the pipe.

Oscar, Jack and Ruby were still staring at the alien. The Slurrisnoat was totally revolting. And very big.

"But it's too far away," said Ruby, "even with these adapted super soakers we'll never hit it."

"Swap places," said Oscar confidently, "I've got an idea."

Ruby and Jack exchanged worried looks. Oscar's ideas were usually dangerous, mucky or both. Oscar saw their looks.

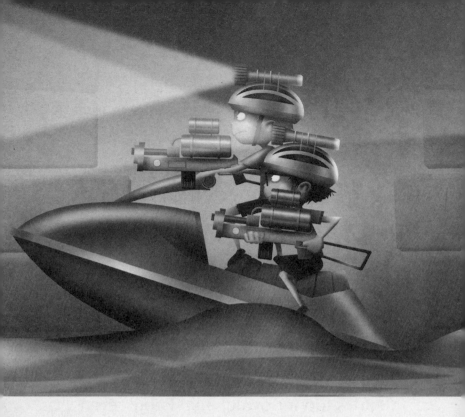

"Come on, give me a chance," he said.

Ruby shrugged and, carefully, swapped places with Oscar.

"Get ready," said Oscar and started up the engine. So far the creature hadn't noticed the three kids but now the engine noise made it turn its head.

Oscar gunned the engine and the jet-ski

shot forward. Jack realised that Oscar's plan
was simple – it was all about speed.

Oscar steered the jet-ski slightly to the right
of the monster and then pulled sharp left. The
jet-ski flew across the front of the alien and
then Oscar killed the engine. All
three children had an excellent
shot right at the creature.

"Whatever you do," screamed Jack, "don't cross the streams!"

"What are you talking about?" asked Ruby.

"Never mind," said Jack, activating his super soaker.

Ruby and Oscar followed suit and soon three powerful blasts of concentrated washing-up liquid were hitting the alien's poo-covered skin. The reaction was incredible. At each point of impact the alien skin blistered and sizzled as if being attacked by acid. The creature began to emit a high-pitched squeal.

The three children kept up the attack, carefully bathing the whole monster in the concentrated washing-up liquid. Finally the super soakers ran dry.

The Slurrisnoat, now completely coated in

the soap, continued to squeal, the sounds
rising in pitch and volume. Its
entire body was smoking and
fizzling. The little hands were

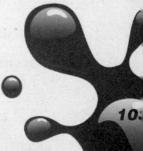

shaking and quivering. In fact, the whole alien was beginning to pulsate.

"Uh-oh," said Snivel, "time to run away..."

Oscar tried to start the engine but it wouldn't fire.

"Out of the way," said Ruby, "there's a trick to it." She clambered back on to the jet-ski and Oscar returned to the platform next to Jack.

The screeching of the Slurrisnoat was now painful to the ears and the alien was now bulging and contracting in a rapid-fire rhythm.

"It's going to blow!" screamed Jack.

Ruby fired up the jet-ski engine and they started to move. Accelerating, she headed for the tunnel they'd originally come from. Behind them the alien exploded, showering the whole hall with tiny bits of blubbery flesh.

Jack cast a glance over his shoulder.

"Oh no!" he said. "That body was just a sort of cocoon."

The true form of the Slurrisnoat was now revealed. It was a giant wasp-like creature with a horrific stinger at the end of its striped body. Using its huge wings to launch into the air, the newly-born Slurrisnoat bore down on the three children.

"Top speed," shouted Jack to Ruby. "Now!"

Zana didn't know what the thing screaming in the tunnels was but it certainly sounded alien to her. With her video camera in one hand she steered her little boat in the direction of the sound.

Something was coming the other way. She could see lights, hear voices, *children's* voices. And something else. Some kind of buzzing?

Suddenly she saw them. A jet-ski pulling a sort of platform behind it and it was heading straight for her! Zana knew she had to try to steer out of the imminent collision but she couldn't move. She was frozen with fear at the sight of the creature that was chasing the children. It was, impossibly, a giant alien wasp.

Zana hated wasps. Really, really hated them, ever since she had been stung by one as a child. And this was the biggest, most frightening

GRASH!

wasp she'd ever seen.

She was so scared she couldn't even scream.

Ruby was also looking at the wasp monster, which was why she didn't see Zana's boat until it was too late.

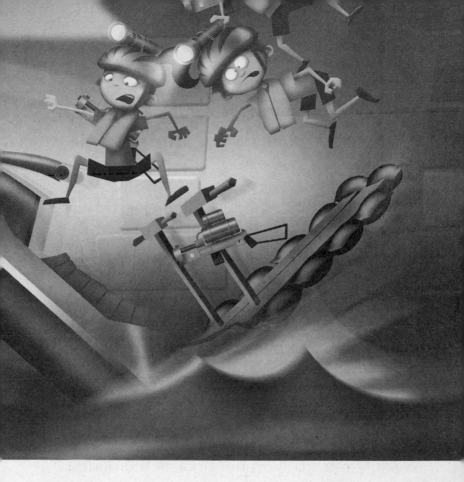

The two craft collided and Zana, Ruby, Oscar, Jack and Snivel were thrown into the air. The inflatable boat did a somersault and landed back on the water and, magically, Jack, Oscar and Ruby landed inside it.

Zana was less lucky.

SPLASH! She landed on her back in the filthy polluted water and then, to add insult to injury, Snivel landed on her chest, dunking her completely in the stinking filth.

The jet-ski itself flew up in a backwards spiral and Jack looked up as, almost in slow motion, it turned in the air before slamming into the Slurrisnoat and knocking the giant wasp back down the tunnel.

The kids looked on in horror as the alien bounced off the tunnel walls a couple of times and then resumed its flight towards them. Only Zana, lying on her back in the sludge with Snivel on her chest, lay between them and the alien.

The alien seemed to have lost a little bit of speed. It must have been injured by the jet-ski, Jack figured. It was still able to fly but much more slowly than before.

For a moment Zana wasn't sure where she was. She was floating and it was almost peaceful. But there was a terrible smell and a dog sitting on her chest and something flying above her... The giant alien wasp! Suddenly

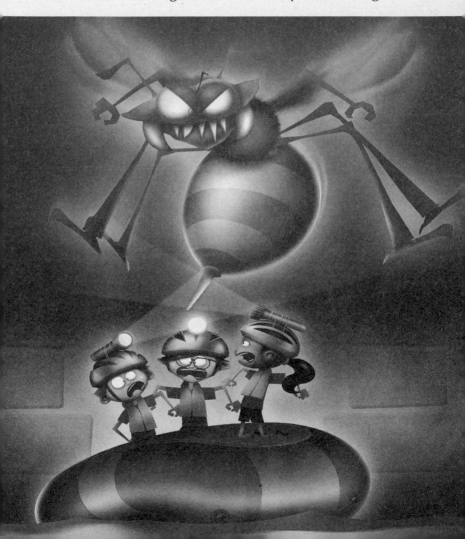

Zana remembered everything and she screamed.

Jack was also screaming. The alien was hovering right over the boat, its stinger quivering!

But the Slurrisnoat was making the most basic mistake of all, without even realising it. Snivel doubled as an alien trap – the only problem being that he had to be directly underneath an alien to be able to catch it.

At least, that was *usually* a problem. Right now the Slurrisnoat was doing their work for them!

The alien darted at Jack with its stinger, but just as the huge barb was about to hit him, he shouted, "**Activate Snivel Trap!**"

Instantly the alien transforming technology inside Snivel activated and he changed shape, becoming a big steel box which sucked the

alien in, like a vacuum cleaner. **SLAM!**
The twin doors on top of the Snivel Trap
slammed shut. **GLINK!** The Blower part
fell onto the Snivel Trap. Zana reached out
and grabbed it automatically.

"We did it!" shouted Jack and
he, Ruby and Oscar gave each
other high fives.

They helped Zana, who seemed to be in an advanced state of shock, back into the boat and secured the Snivel Trap. Ruby took the controls and steered them back into the open air. Jack had never been so relieved to be outside and breathing in the lovely scents of summer – the freshly mown grass, the flowers,

the clean water of the river.

"Now what?" said Oscar.

"Better text Bob and make our delivery," said Jack getting out his mobile phone.

He quickly tapped out a message and pressed *send*.

The boat was now back on the river. Zana had fallen into a twitchy sleep and Ruby had taken off her jacket to put over the woman. Oscar and Jack sighed.

"I guess it's all over now," said Oscar.

Jack nodded. "Suppose so."

Ruby looked back at them. "At least the Earth's safe now."

Then, without warning, a blue light appeared out of nowhere and descended over the boat.

Jack felt a really odd sensation, as if he was weightless.

Zana opened her eyes. There was a blue light pulsating somewhere. Was it the police again? She sat up and was just in time to see the three children and the metal box that had once been a dog fade away into the night sky as if they had never been there.

Zana was all alone in the boat, floating along the river, with nothing but a girl's jacket and clothes soaked in the most disgusting water known to man to show for her adventure.

Zana began to sob. Life really was unfair.

cHÅPTER EIGHT

Jack opened his eyes and realised with a start that he wasn't on the boat any more. He was sprawled on a cold concrete floor. Nearby Oscar and Ruby were also stirring. Jack got to his feet and found that he was a little bit wobbly on them.

"That's usual when you've been in a teleport beam," said a familiar voice. "But the dizziness

will wear off in a moment."

"Bob?!" asked Jack.

"That's me!" said a man standing near by. He was short, slightly overweight, and had one of those half-hearted beards that adults call goatees. He was dressed in a cheap-looking suit that was possibly a size too small for him. He was wide-eyed and a little sweaty.

Jack wasn't sure exactly what he had thought Bob would look like but it wasn't anything like this. This man looked more like a nervous supply teacher than a GUNGE agent.

"Is this it?" asked Jack. "Gunge HQ?"

"It's my base," said Bob. "I didn't want to waste any more time so I teleported you directly here. Takes a huge amount of energy though. Most of the town will be without electricity for the next twenty-four hours, but I'm sure they'll cope."

Ruby and Oscar
got to their feet
and stood a
little closer to
Jack. They
watched in
silence as Bob
aimed what
looked like a TV
remote control at the
Snivel Trap. A blue light appeared from the
remote and engulfed the steel box, which then
faded from view.

"What have you done with Snivel?"

"Come with me – I'll show you," said Bob.
He led the three slightly subdued children
through a door into a dark corridor. As they
followed him along the
passageway they became
aware of glass-fronted cells on

each side. Four were illuminated.

"That's the Squillibloat," said Oscar pointing at the first illuminated cage. The first monster they had captured was asleep inside his cell, looking far less dangerous than when they had first seen it.

"And there's the Burrapong we found at the zoo," said Ruby as they reached the second lit room.

"And here's the Flartibug," said Jack as they passed the third of the rooms.

Finally they came to the fourth illuminated cell where their latest victim – the Slurrisnoat – was buzzing around angrily, zapping the glass wall with its stinger to little effect. Bob pressed a control and thick white gas began to pump into the room. The Slurrisnoat stopped banging the glass and tried to fly closer to the ceiling to escape the gas but it was no good. Slowly the creature lost

consciousness and it fell heavily to the floor.
Even though it was a deadly, man-eating
alien the children couldn't help but feel a little
bit sorry for it.

"You've killed it," said Ruby.

"No, of course not, it's just sedated. Like the
others it'll be put into suspended animation,
for security reasons," explained Bob.

"And then what? I suppose your GUNGE scientists will cut it up and conduct horrible experiments on it?" asked Jack, not liking what he was seeing.

"I'm sure that's not going to happen," said Bob unconvincingly. "Right then, come on, let's see the rest of our trophies."

He led them to the end of the corridor where the four parts of the Blower that the children had collected were sitting on lit platforms on a special display unit. Snivel was also there, back in his dog form, waiting for them. Pleased to see his master, he hurried over to join Jack and his friends.

"Isn't it dangerous having all the bits in the same place?" asked Oscar. "Like having all your eggs in one basket?"

Bob shook his head. "No, no, no. It's perfectly safe in our hands. In fact now you're here, perhaps you can work out how to put it together. It's a bit of a puzzle."

"I'm not really good at puzzles," said Oscar.

"Me neither," said Ruby.

Bob turned to Jack and smiled. "What about you?"

Jack shrugged.

Bob started passing him the bits of Blower.

"Come on now, Jack. You're meant to be a genius inventor. You're always putting things together, aren't you? A simple bit of alien tech like this isn't going to defeat you, is it?"

Jack started looking at the pieces, the challenge beginning to interest him despite his reservations. The pieces no longer resembled the things Jack and his friends had recovered from the aliens – glowing earrings and necklaces. Now they were strange pieces of metal that seemed to have too many sides, and made Jack's head hurt a bit.

"Are you sure it's safe?" he asked, turning one of the pieces round and round in his hands.

"It won't hurt you, if that's what you mean..." said Bob in almost a whisper.

Almost without consciously thinking about it Jack connected two of the pieces together. They slid into place soundlessly and left him with a odd shaped construct that didn't look as if it had ever been anything but one single piece.

"Oh, you are good," said Bob, clearly impressed.

"He's the best," said Oscar loyally.

"I can see that," said Bob.

Jack was now examining the third piece. Like the first two this had changed shape from when it was first taken and now took the form of a multi-sided shape with odd angles. Jack turned it round and round, feeling

the shape with his
fingers. Then with a
sudden move he
brought the new
piece into contact
with the first two,
twisted, clicked,
twisted in the other
direction and then there

was just one bigger piece in his hands.

Bob handed him the last segment. "Just this
one now."

Jack looked at it carefully. It had odd
curves to it and a long spiky bit – but where
on the larger part could it go? Jack held the
large part up to the light and turned it around
in his fingers, looking at it from every angle.
And then he saw it. Click! Twist!
Clunk! It was done.

The Blower was complete.

Jack turned it in his hands. It looked like a sort of electronic horn now, with a mouthpiece where you could put your lips and blow.

"Thank you," said Bob, plucking the Blower from Jack's hands. "I was having a real problem working out how to do that."

"But what are you going to do with it? More tests and experiments?" demanded Jack.

"You could say that," replied Bob with a nasty grin. He began to raise the Blower to his lips.

"Bob! What are you doing?" cried Jack.

Bob stopped and looked at Jack. He shook his head sadly.

"You know, for a genius, you really are a very stupid boy sometimes. Haven't you worked it out yet? I am what's known technically as a turncoat, a traitor, a double agent. The four GUNK Alien races are just a

few of the alien species out there who would love Earth's snot. Some of them contacted me and made me an offer I couldn't refuse."

"Offer? What kind of offer?" asked Jack.

"When the aliens take over I will be King of the Planet. I'm going to rule the world. And everyone else on it... will just be fuel!"

Bob put the Blower to his lips and blew long and hard.

Jack, Oscar and Ruby just stared at him, mouths hanging open in complete astonishment.

Bob pulled the Blower from his lips and grinned at them coldly.

"Right, that should do it. They're on their way. The aliens are coming. And there's not a thing you or anyone else can do about it."